The Satyricon
Dinner with Trimalchio

PETRONIUS

translated by
R. BRACHT BRANHAM
and
DANIEL KINNEY

A Phoenix Paperback

This abridged edition of Petronius' *Satyricon*
published in 1996 by Phoenix
a division of Orion Books Ltd
Orion House, 5 Upper St Martin's Lane, London WC2H 9EA

Translation copyright © J. M. Dent 1996

Cover illustration: Gabrielle d'Estrees and her sister, the Duchess of Villars,
late 16th century by Fontainebleau School (Giraudon/Bridgeman Art
Library, London)

ISBN 1 85799 565 1

Typeset by Deltatype Ltd, Ellesmere Port, Cheshire
Printed in Great Britain by Clays Ltd, St Ives plc

Dinner With Trimalchio

The third day had already arrived, and that meant the prospect of a free meal. But we were so tattered and bruised we felt more like running away than resting. While we morosely pondered how to avoid the coming storm, one of Agamemnon's slaves interrupted us: 'What's wrong? Don't you know who your host is today? It's Trimalchio, a most elegant man . . . He has a water clock in his dining room and a trumpeter on call to announce the time, so that he knows at any moment how much of life he's already lost.'

We promptly forgot all our troubles, dressed up, and asked Giton, who so willingly played the servant's role, to accompany us to the baths . . .

While we wandered the grounds in our evening clothes – or rather joked around and mingled with groups of guests playing games – we suddenly encountered a bald old man in a blood-red tunic playing ball with some long-haired boys. It was not so much the boys who caught our attention – although they were well worth it – as the paterfamilias himself. He stood there in his slippers playing intently with a

1

leek-green ball. If the ball hit the ground, he didn't chase it, but had a slave with a bag full of balls give the players a new one. We noticed some other novelties: there were two eunuchs stationed at different points in a circle; one was holding a silver chamber pot, the other was counting the balls – not those batted back and forth by the players, but only those that fell on the ground!

While we wondered at the extravagance of all this, Menelaus ran up and said, '*This* is the guy who's throwing the party! What you see is only the prelude to dinner.' As Menelaus spoke, Trimalchio snapped his fingers as a signal to the eunuch to hold out the chamber pot for him as he continued to play. After emptying his bladder, he called for water for his hands, sprinkled it lightly on his fingers and then wiped them dry on the head of a young slave . . .

There wasn't time to take it all in, so we entered the baths, and the minute we began to sweat moved on to the cold pool. Trimalchio was already drenched in perfume and being towelled down, not with linen, but with Greek comforters of the softest wool. Right in front of him three masseurs were guzzling a fine Falernian wine. When they proceeded to spill most of it in a scuffle, he blithely observed that this was 'a libation in his honor'.

He was then wrapped in a scarlet cloak and placed upon a litter. Four runners bristling with decorations pranced before him along with a little wagon on which his darling was riding – a boy past his prime, puffy eyed, and even uglier than his master. As Trimalchio was being carried out, a musician holding a tiny flute ran up to his side and – just as if he were whispering a secret in his ear – played for him the whole way!

Utterly astonished, we made our way to the door with Agamemnon. By the entrance we saw a notice posted:

ANY SLAVE WHO LEAVES THE PREMISES WITHOUT
PERMISSION OF THE MASTER
WILL RECEIVE ONE HUNDRED LASHES

Just inside stood a doorman dressed entirely in green except for a cherry-red belt around his waist. He was shucking peas into a silver dish. Over the doorsill hung a golden cage from which a motley-colored magpie called salutations to the guests.

While I stared in stupefaction at all this, I almost fell over backwards and broke a leg. For just to the left of the entrance (not far from the porter's lodge), was the most enormous dog tethered by a chain – painted on the wall under some large block letters that said:

BEWARE OF DOG

My companions laughed at my fright, but I pulled myself together to look at the rest of the wall. It depicted a slave market complete with price tags. Trimalchio himself was in the picture: his hair is long and in his hand he grips the wand of Mercury. Minerva leads the way as our hero enters Rome. A painstaking artist had carefully portrayed the whole course

3

of his career, complete with captions: how he first learned to keep the books and then was put in charge of the cash. In the last scene of the fresco Mercury lifts him by the chin up to a lofty dais. Fortuna is at his side carrying her burgeoning cornucopia, as the three Fates spin the golden threads.

I also noticed a team of runners in the nearby colonnade exercising with their trainer. In the corner stood an imposing cabinet: inside I saw a little shrine containing the household gods sculpted in silver, a marble statuette of Venus, and a none-too-small golden casket, which, they said, preserved the master's first beard . . .

I started to ask the steward what they had painted in the atrium. 'The *Iliad* and the *Odyssey*,' he said, 'and the gladiator show put on by Laenas.' It was too much to contemplate . . .

We had already reached the dining room. In the entryway a book-keeper was poring over the accounts. But what caught my eye were the rods and axes fixed on the doorposts. They were mounted on top of what looked like the bronze prow of a ship that bore the inscription:

PRESENTED TO C. POMPEIUS TRIMALCHIO
PRIEST OF THE COLLEGE OF AUGUSTUS
BY CINNAMUS THE STEWARD

Beneath this inscription was a double lamp suspended from the ceiling and two wooden tablets, one on each doorpost. I seem to rememberd that one of them read:

On the other were painted the phases of the moon and images of the seven planets, and lucky and unlucky days were marked with studs of different colors.

When we had had enough of these diversions and were ready to enter the dining room, a slave – evidently assigned this job – shouted, 'Right foot first!' We were momentarily taken aback for fear one of us should commit some faux pas as he entered the room. But just as we moved our right feet forward in unison, a slave stripped for flogging threw himself at our feet and begged us to save him! He was only guilty of a minor offense, it seemed: the book-keeper's clothes had been stolen from him at the baths. They were only worth a pittance. We drew back our right feet and begged a pardon from the book-keeper as he sat there counting gold pieces in the hallway. He looked up like royalty and said, 'It is not the financial loss that irks me, but the sheer negligence of this worthless slave! He lost *my* dress clothes, a birthday present from a client, dyed of course in the finest Tyrian purple. Admittedly they had been washed once. Well, what can I say? You can have him!'

Grateful for the book-keeper's munificence, we now entered the dining room. Then the slave we had just saved ran up and, before we knew what had hit us, smothered us in kisses and thanked us effusively for our kindness. 'Listen,' he whispered, 'you'll see in a minute who it is you've befriended: the master's wine, courtesy of your waiter!'

At last we took our places. Some Alexandrian slave-boys poured melted snow over our hands, while others tended our feet, meticulously paring our hangnails. Not even this distasteful task was done in silence: they kept singing as they worked. I wanted to find out whether the entire household sang, so I ordered a drink. A most attentive slave promptly responded in a grating soprano. In fact, every request was answered in song. You would have thought you were in a pantomime, not a formal dining room. Nonetheless, they served great antipasto. Everyone was now in their place except for Trimalchio, who, following the current fashion, had reserved the most prominent seat for himself.

On the hors d'oeuvres tray stood a donkey of Corinthian bronze bearing saddlebags stuffed with olives, white in one side, black in the other. Two platters flanked the animal; their weight in silver and Trimalchio's name were engraved along their edges. Little bridges welded to the plate supported dormice sprinkled with honey and poppyseeds. There were even sausages sizzling on a silver gridiron, which arched over some Syrian plums and pomegranate seeds.

We were in the midst of these delicacies when Trimalchio was carried in to a fanfare of trumpets and placed amid a veritable fortress of cushions – a sight that elicited some indiscreet laughter from the guests. For his shaven head poked out of a scarlet shawl, and round his muffled neck he had tucked a napkin bearing a stripe of senatorial purple and a fringe of tassels that dangled here and there. On the smallest finger of his left hand he wore a huge gilded ring. On the very last joint of the next finger he wore a smaller ring that appeared to be pure gold, but actually was studded with little iron stars. But his display of wealth didn't stop there; he exposed his right biceps, which was adorned with a golden armlet and a bangle of ivory fastened by a bright metal clasp.

After picking his teeth with a silver toothpick, he began: 'Friends, I really wasn't in the mood to come to dinner yet; but rather than keep you waiting, I have denied myself every pleasure. At least allow me to finish my game.'

A slave followed with a board of terebinth and a pair of crystal dice. Then I noticed the most extravagant touch yet: instead of the usual white and black counting-stones, he had substituted coins of gold and silver. While he chattered away over his game and we tasted the hors d'oeuvres, a tray was served with a basket on it. There sat a wooden hen with her wings spread out in a circle, just as they do when they're hatching eggs. Two slaves immediately came up and, as the music blared on, began to search through the straw. Peahens' eggs were found and promptly distributed to the guests.

Trimalchio looked over at this scene and said, 'Friends, I had peahens' eggs placed under the chicken. But to tell the truth, I'm afraid they may have already been fertilized! Let's try them and see if they can still be sucked.'

We picked up our spoons – weighing no less than half a

pound each – and poked at the eggs, which were encased in fine pastry. I was about to throw mine away, because it already seemed to have a chick inside it. Then I overheard a more experienced guest remark, 'I'll bet there's something good in here!' So I pushed my finger through the shell and found the fattest little fig-pecker marinated in peppered egg yolk.

Since his game was now interrupted, Trimalchio had ordered all the same dishes for himself and announced in a loud voice that whoever wanted a second glass of aperitif could have one. Then, suddenly, a musical cue was given and all at once our hors d'oeuvres were whisked away by a chorus of singing slaves. Amid all the commotion one of the dishes was accidentally dropped and a slave retrieved it from the floor. Trimalchio noticed this, had the servant's ears boxed, and ordered him to throw the dish back on the floor. A house slave appeared and began to sweep up the silverware along with the rest of the mess. Then two long-haired Ethiopians came in holding little wineskins – like those used to dampen the sand at the amphitheatre – and they poured wine over our hands. No one even offered water.

When complimented on his elegant service, Trimalchio replied, 'Mars loves a level playing field. So I've had each guest assigned his own table. And that way the bustle of these smelly slaves won't bother us so.'

Carefully sealed wine bottles were promptly served; attached to their necks were labels:

FALERNIAN WINE
BOTTLED IN THE CONSULSHIP OF OPIMIUS
ONE HUNDRED YEARS OLD

While we were studying the labels, Trimalchio clapped his hands together and cried, 'How sad! Even a bottle of wine outlives a mere man. So, let's wet our whistles, friends. Wine is life – and *this* wine's real Opimian! I didn't serve anything this good yesterday, and the guests were much classier.'

We were drinking the wine and thoroughly relishing all the luxuries of the feast when a slave brought in a silver skeleton so loosely jointed that its limbs swivelled in every direction. He promptly threw it down on the table several times. Each time its floppy limbs fell in a different pattern. Trimalchio responded in verse:

> 'Alas! Poor us! We all add up to squat;
> once Hades gets his hooks in, that's the lot;
> so live while it's your turn, 'cause then it's not.'

Our applause was followed by a dish that was disappointingly small, but so odd it had everyone staring at it. On a round serving tray the twelve signs of the zodiac were arranged in a circle. Over each sign the specialty chef had placed the kind of food that fit its character: over Aries the ram, a ramifying pea; on Taurus the bull, a slice of rump roast; over Gemini the twins, testicles and kidneys; on the Crab, a crown of flowers; over the Lion, a virile African fig; on Virgo, the womb of a barren sow; over Libra, a set of scales with a cheesetart on one side, balanced by a pancake on the other; on Scorpio, ... [the scorpion fish]; on Sagittarius, a seahorse; on Capricorn, a lobster; on Aquarius, a goose; on Pisces, a pair of snapper. In the middle of all this was a piece of turf, torn out roots and all, with a honeycomb sitting on it. An Egyptian slave boy was bringing bread around in a silver chafing dish . . . while the master himself belted out a tune from the mime, *The North African Quack*, in a hideous voice.

We were looking gloomily at this vile fare when Trimalchio piped up, 'Please, let's eat! This is just the preamble to our dinner!'

As he spoke, four male dancers bounced up in time to the music and snatched the lid off the next dish. Inside we saw some fowl and sows' udders and a hare adorned with wings to look like Pegasus. At the corners of the dish we noticed four little statues of Marsyas the satyr; from their wineskins a pepper sauce poured over fish that looked as if they were swimming in a little canal. We all joined in the applause started by the slaves, and, grinning broadly, proceeded to attack the choicest items.

And Trimalchio, no less amused by such tricks, called out, 'Carver!' A butcher instantly appeared and, waving his arms to the beat of the music, sliced up the meat. You would have thought of a charioteer fighting to the sound of a water organ. Trimalchio kept egging him on, muttering under his breath, 'Carv-er! Carv-er!' Suspecting that some joke was being played, I wasn't embarrassed to ask the man next to me what he thought. An old hand at these games, he said, 'You see that guy who's carving the fish up? His name is "Carver". So every time Trimalchio says the word "Carver", he's both calling his name and giving him orders!'

I couldn't eat another bite. So I turned to my table companion to turn up as much as I could. I started to pump him for stories, and began by asking who that woman was bustling up and down the dining room.

'Trimalchio's wife,' he said. 'Her name's Fortunata, and she counts her money by the ton! And what was she the day before yesterday? Well, if I may be frank, you wouldn't have touched her bread from her hand. But now – god knows how or why – she's in hog heaven and Trimalchio revolves around her. Listen, if she said day was night, he'd believe it. Trimalchio himself is so filthy rich he doesn't even know what he owns. But this bitch knows it all in advance, gets there first every time. She's a dry one, sober and savvy – you see all the gold, don't you? But she has a vicious tongue – a real household hellcat. If she likes you, she likes you; if she doesn't, well, she doesn't. And Trimalchio? His estates run as far as the crow flies – money makes money! He has more silver lying around his porter's lodge than other guys have in their entire fortunes. And slaves? Holy shit, I don't think even one in ten knows who owns him. Listen, he could buy and sell one of these young hot shots here without even noticing it.

'Not that he buys anything. Everything is home grown:

wool, lemons, pepper – you name it. You want hen's milk? You got it. For example, his wool wasn't good enough for him. He bought some rams from south Italy and turned them loose on his flock. He wanted home-grown Attic honey, so he had some bees brought over from Athens; that way even the native bees get better. Why, just the other day he placed an order for mushroom spores – from India! He won't even own a mule unless it was sired by a wild ass! See all these cushions – even the stuffing is dyed purple or scarlet! Now that's what I call happy!

'But don't look down your nose at these other ex-slaves here. They're loaded. You see that guy at the end of the last table? He's got eight hundred grand. He started with nothing. In fact, he used to schlep wood around on his back. Anyway, they say – I don't know, what I *heard* was – that he snatched the cap off a gnome and found his treasure! I don't begrudge anyone a godsend. But now that he's been slapped into freedom, he wants a good time. He put a sign on his old place saying:

GARRET OF C. POMPEIUS DIOGENES
AVAILABLE TO LET FROM THE FIRST OF JULY:
HE OWNS HIS OWN HOUSE NOW

For that matter the guy in the freedman's seat there had it laid in the shade – not that I blame him. He had his hands on a million and dropped the ball. Now I don't think he owns his own hair! It's not his fault, god knows. You'll never meet a nicer guy. Some damned freedmen made a killing at his expense. You know how it goes: you have partners, so your pot never boils, and when the business craters out, your friends vanish. What a righteous business he had, and look at him now! He was an undertaker.

'He used to eat like a king too – boars roasted whole, fancy pastry, poultry – his own cooks and bakers. He spilled more wine on his floor than other guys keep in their cellars. A legend in his own mind. When his business went bust and he was afraid his creditors would catch on to the mess he was in, he put up an auction notice like this:

FOR SALE:
SOME UNNEEDED ASSETS,
CONTACT C. IULIUS PROCULUS'

Trimalchio interrupted his charming story; for the second course had now been removed, and the guests were buoyed up by the wine and engrossed in conversation. Leaning on his elbow, our host began, 'I hope you're doing justice to this wine. Fish gotta swim! Tell me, did you really think I'd be satisfied with those signs of the zodiac you saw served on that covered serving-dish? "Is that the Ulysses you know?" What's that? You mustn't forget your classics, even at dinner! May the bones of my old master rest in peace; he wanted me to be a man among men. So nobody can teach me anything new; the clear proof is this *fête accomplie*.

'Heaven here, where the twelve gods dwell, turns into the same number of signs. First, there is Aries, the Ram. Whoever is born under the Ram has many flocks, lots of wool, a 13 shameless rug, a hard head, and a horny noggin. Under this sign are born many scholars and other boneheads.'

We commended our astrologer's wit, and so he continued: 'Then the whole sky changes into Taurus, the Bull. So bullheaded types are born, and cattlemen, and people who look out for number one. Now under Gemini pairs are born, horses and oxen, ballsy fellows, and people who like it both ways. I was born under Cancer. So I have many legs to stand on, and I have many possessions on land and sea. Either way fits a crab! That's why I didn't put anything on top of the crab – so I wouldn't weigh down my sign! Under the Lion piggy eaters and bossy people are born. Under Virgo come sissies, runaway slaves, and candidates for a chain gang. Under the Scales come butchers, perfumers, and whoever weighs things up for a living. Under Scorpio, you get poisoners and assassins. Under Sagittarius are the shifty-eyed types who squint at the vegetables and pocket the bacon. Under Capricorn are people in trouble who worry so much they sprout little horns. Under Aquarius, the Water-Bearer, come bartenders and people with water on the brain. Under Pisces are fishmongers and rhetoricians.

'So the whole world whirls around just like a millstone, and it's always up to no good, what with people getting born or dying. And that dirt clod you saw in the middle – with the honeycomb on top? That was no accident. Everything I do has a reason: mother earth is in the middle of all, round as an egg, and she has all good things inside her, like a honeycomb.'

'Brilliant!' we cry in a single voice, and with our hands raised towards the ceiling, we swear that the great astronomers Hipparchus and Aratus were nothing compared to him. Meanwhile servants came in and in front of our couches spread out embroidered coverlets depicting men with nets and spears poised in their hands, and the whole drama of the hunt. We still didn't know what to expect when we heard an awful racket in the next room, and lo and behold, a pack of Spartan hunting dogs started to charge around our table! They were followed by a serving tray carrying a wild boar of the most enormous proportions with a little cap of freedom perched on its head. From its tusks dangled baskets woven from palm leaves – one full of fresh Syrian dates, the other of dried Egyptian dates. Little piglets made of cake were placed around the boar as if they were hanging on its teats, so we would think we had a sow before us. These were actually gifts to take home.

The boar was not carved by the inimitable Carver – who had massacred the fowl – but by a huge bearded man decked out in leggings and a fancy striped hunting jacket. He proceeded to draw a hunting knife and plunge it into the boar's side as if his life depended on it; out of the gash he made exploded a covey of quail. Fowlers were ready with their reeds and quickly caught the birds as they flew about the dining room. Trimalchio gave orders that everyone should be served his own bird and then remarked facetiously, 'Would you take a look at the acorns that boar's been dining on in the forest!' Two young slaves instantly stepped up to the baskets hanging from the boar's tusks and distributed the Theban and Syrian dates equally among the guests.

Meanwhile I was wondering to myself why on earth that boar had come in with a freedom cap on its head. After imagining all kinds of nonsense, I ventured to tell my 'guide' what was puzzling me. He replied, 'Even your humble servant could figure that one out. It's no puzzle – it's plain as day. The boar was ordered for the main course yesterday, but the guests chose to let it go, so it comes back to the banquet today just like a "freed-man"!' I cursed my stupidity and asked no more questions: I didn't want them to think I'd never dined in good company!

While we were talking, a beautiful boy wearing a wreath of vine leaves and ivy brought around a little basket of grapes and pretended to be Dionysus in his various guises: first, he was Bromius the Roarer, then Lyaeus the Liberator, and Euhius the Reveller. He also served up his master's lyrics in a piercing soprano. Trimalchio turned around at the sound and said, 'Dionysus, be Liberated.' The boy promptly took the cap of freedom off the boar's head and put it on his own. Then Trimalchio quipped, 'You can't deny that I have a Free Father!' We applauded Trimalchio's bon mot and gave the boy a wet kiss when he came by.

After this course Trimalchio got up to go to the toilet. Free of our imperious host we began to incite the guests to conversation. Dama was the first to talk after calling for another round of wine: 'A day's nothin'. Before ya can turn around it's night. So nothin's better than goin' straight from bed to dinner. An' its been downright frigid lately. A bath hardly thaws me out. But a hot drink's as good as a warm coat! I've been drinking by the jug, and I'm sloshed. The wine's gone right to my brain.'

Seleucus then joined in the conversation: 'Now, I don't take a bath every day, the water's got a bite to it and melts your insides – it's like gettin' launder'd every day! But when I've just downed a jug of spiced wine, I tell Mr Cold to "fuck off, please". Couldn't even take a bath anyway – had to go to a funeral today. A swell guy, good old Chrysanthus has blown his last bubble. I ran into him just the other day, ya know. I can almost see myself talking to him . . . Goddamn pitiful, ain't it? We're just walking windbags. Worse'n flies; even flies got somethin' to 'em, but we're not worth a goddamn bubble!

'And what if Chrysanthus hadn't tried that strict starvation diet? Not a crumb of bread or drop of water touched his lips for five days! Now he's joined the silent majority. His doctors killed him – no, it was just plain bad luck. The doctors are just there to cheer us up on the way out. Anyway, it was a nice funeral – first-rate casket, nice lining and all. And what a loud crowd of mourners – except for his wife (he'd obviously freed some slaves to swell the crowd). And what if he wasn't the greatest husband in the world? Women and vultures: the same animal, ain't it? Don't do a woman no favors. Might as well chuck it down a well. 17

Yeah, an old love is an old sore.'

This guy was getting to be a bore. Phileros interjected loudly, 'Let us remember the living! Your friend has balanced his books: he lived a decent life and died the same way. What's there to complain about? He started with a nickel in his pocket and was always ready to pluck a dime out of the dung with his teeth. So whatever he touched grew like a honeycomb. By god, I'll bet he left a hundred thousand "free and clear", all in hard cash. To tell the truth – since I've got a bit of the Cynic in me – he had a big mouth and a vicious tongue – a walking quarrel, not a man. His brother, on the other hand, was brave, loyal, open-handed and hospitable. But Chrysanthus got started on the wrong foot, until his first vintage set him right. He could name his price for that wine. What kept his head above water was that he came into an inheritance – and stole more than was left him. Then, the jerk left the money to some nobody because he was mad at his own brother! Whoever runs out on his family has to run a long way. Then he trusted those slaves who ruined him. Businessmen can't afford to be gullible. But he enjoyed what he had while he had it . . . You only get what's given, not what you aim for. He was a lucky dog; lead turned to gold in his hands. It's easy when everything runs along, fair and square. How old do you think he was? Over seventy. He was hard as nails, carried his age well, and his hair was black as a crow. I knew the guy for years and years, and he was still horny. By god, I don't think a dog was safe in his house! What's more, he still went in for boys too – a real jack of all trades. Not that I blame him – that's all he took with him.'

This was Phileros, and Ganymede followed: 'What on earth are you goin' on about? Don't you care how the price of corn is pinching us? Goddamnit, I couldn't even find a bite of bread this morning! And how this drought drags on. We've already been starvin' a whole year. Damn those bureaucrats! They're makin' deals with the bakers: "You scratch my back and I'll scratch yours." So the little guy slaves away and the fat cats live like every day's the Saturnalia. If we only had some real men around, like the kind I found here when I arrived from Asia.

'Now those were the days . . . they used to knock the holy tar out of corrupt officials – put the fear of god in 'em. I still remember Safinius. He used to live down by the old arch when I was a boy. A hot pepper, not a man: Yeah, he used to singe the ground with his feet. But he was honest, reliable, a loyal friend – you could play how-many-fingers with him in the dark. And how he used to lay into some of them on the town council – he didn't beat around the bush, he attacked head-on. When he was pleading a case in court, his voice boomed like a tuba. He didn't sweat or spit much either – I guess he was just blessed by the gods. He always had a friendly word for you, knew everybody's name, was just like one of us. So, food was cheap as dirt then. You could buy more bread for a penny than you and your buddy could choke down. I've seen bull's-eyes bigger than the loaves they sell now.

'Shit, it's getting worse every day. This town's got it all ass backwards. Why do we have this mayor who's not worth a fig? He'd sell us down the river for small change. He sits there at home, happy as a clam; pockets more money in a day than most of us have in the bank. (I happen to know where he got a grand in cash.) If we had any balls, we'd wipe that smile off his face. Nowadays, everyone's a lion at home, a fox on the street.

'Take me, I've already eaten my rags; if food prices stay up, I'll have to sell my little cottage. What's gonna happen to us if neither gods nor men take pity on this town? And I'll be damn'd if it's not all the gods' doin'. No one believes heaven is heaven these days. No one fasts. No one gives a fig for Jove. Instead, they bow their heads to count their profits. In the old days mothers used to climb the hill to pray for rain in long robes and bare feet with their hair down and their minds pure – and it poured buckets! It was now or never. And everyone used to come home looking like drowned rats. If the gods are angry, it's because we're not religious any more. Our fields just lie there—'

'Hey!' blurted out Echion, the ragman, 'watch what you say – it's bad luck. If it ain't one thing, it's another – like the yokel said when he lost his spotted pig. What today isn't, tomorrow will be. And so it goes. By god, you couldn't name a better town than this, if we only had the men. Sure, times are hard – and not just here. We shouldn't be too persnickety though – we all live under the same sky. If you were anywhere else, you'd say the pigs walk around here already roasted!

'And listen, in a couple of days we're gonna have a swell fight at the festival, and not just an old troupe of gladiators either but lots of freedmen too. Our Titus has a big heart and likes to go whole hog. This will be the real thing, whatever he does: I'm one of his people, ya know, and he doesn't do anything halfway. He'll put on a great fight with no mercy: a regular butcher's shop right in the middle, where everybody can really see it. After all, he's got the dough; he came into a bundle when his old man died. Tough luck! He could spend half a million and not even miss it. And his name'll go down in history. He's already got some dwarfs, a woman charioteer and Glyco's steward – who was caught in the act of givin' the missus a good time. You'll see the crowd split – the jealous husbands versus the back-door men. Hell, Glyco's not worth a red penny and he's feedin' his own man to the bears! Guess who's been cuckolded? Now, whose fault's that? A slave's just follow-in' orders. Now that latrine of a wife ought to get the bull's horns! But whoever can't beat his donkey, slaughters his saddle. Why did Glyco think that weedy daughter of Hermogenes would ever be worth a damn? Hermogenes himself could steal the feathers off a bird in flight! You can't make a snake into rope. And Glyco? He's doin' in his own people! As long as he lives he'll be branded, till Orcus blots it out. But we all have to make our own mistakes. 21

'I can almost taste what Mammaea's gonna give us to eat – two bits apiece for me and mine. And if he does, he'll sure steal the show from Norbanus. Lemme tell ya, we're gonna win hands down. After all, what has Norbanus ever done for us? He put on some two-bit gladiators so decrepit they'd fall over if you blew on 'em. I've seen better bear-bait. He killed some horsemen that looked like lamp decorations – you'd have thought 'em a bunch of barnyard roosters! One looked like the stick you'd use to beat a mule, another had a club-foot and the third-stringer – who was crippled – looked already dead! There was one Thracian with some guts, but even he fought by the rules. Of course, they were flogged afterwards. All they heard from the crowd was, "Let 'em have it!" What a bunch of cowards.

' "Still, I put on a show for you," says Norbanus. And for that I give him a hand, which is more than he gave us. Add it up. One hand washes another.

'Agamemnon, I'll bet you're thinkin': "What is this clown yammerin' on about?" You're the one who knows how to talk, but you ain't talkin'. You're not like us – you think the way us poor men talk is funny. We know you're just crazy about words, Mr Professor – so what? Can't I still get you to come down to my house someday and see my little place? We'll find something to eat – a chicken, some eggs. It'll be swell, even if the weather has dried up damn near everything! We'll find a way to get full.

'My boy, ya know, is already growin' into one of your

pupils. He even knows his fractions! If he survives, you'll have a little slave at your side. His head's over that writing tablet every time he's got a chance. He's clever; there's something to him – even if he is half crazy over birds. I just killed his three finches and told him a weasel ate them. He's already discovered some other foolery: he likes to paint plenty. Still, he's got a toehold in Greek and is beginning to take to Latin, even if his teacher is a show-off and won't stick to the subject. He knows his stuff, just don't like to work. Now the boy's other tutor isn't exactly educated, but he's thorough – teaches more than he knows! He even keeps coming on holidays, and he's happy with whatever you give him!

'Now I've bought the boy some law books. I wanted him to get a taste of law for home use: there's bread in it. He's spoiled enough by literature. But if he doesn't take to it, I'm gonna teach him a trade, as a barber, or an auctioneer, or a lawyer, at least – something they can't take away from ya till the day ya die. Every day I drum it into him: "Primigenius, believe me, whatever ya learn, ya learn for yourself. Ya see Phileros, the lawyer? If he hadn't studied, he'd be starvin'. It was just the other day when he used to lug a flea-market around on his back! Now he can even sue Norbanus!" Yessir, learnin's a treasure, and a trade never starves.'

The air was buzzing with talk like this when Trimalchio waltzed in, mopped his brow, washed his hands in some scented water, and, after pausing a moment, said: 'My friends, forgive me, but my stomach has been unresponsive 23 for many days. The doctors are lost. Nonetheless, a concoction of pomegranate rind mixed with pine sap boiled in vinegar has loosened things up a bit. I hope my stomach remembers its manners now; otherwise it's as noisy as a bull. And if anyone of you wants to relieve himself, there's nothing to be ashamed about. None of us was ever born solid inside. I don't think there's any greater torment than holding yourself in. This is the one thing Jove himself cannot deny us. Are you smiling, Fortunata, when your stomach keeps me awake all night?

'I don't object to your doing anything here in the dining room if it makes you feel better. Even doctors forbid holding it in. And if more comes out than you expected, well, there are facilities just outside – water, chamber pots, and little sponges. Believes me, those vapors go right into your brain and upset the whole body. I personally know many, many men who've died because they wouldn't admit the truth to themselves.'

We complimented him on his enlightened attitude, and drowned our laughter in our glasses. We didn't know yet that we were only 'half way up the hill', as the saying goes. The tables were cleared to the sound of music and three white pigs were led in wearing halters and little bells. The headwaiter said one was two years old, another three, and the third almost six. I thought some acrobats had arrived and the pigs would perform some amazing stunts, as they do in street shows. This expectation was dispelled when Trimalchio asked:

'Which one do you want for dinner right now? Any slob can turn out a roast chicken, some minestrone, or other trifles; my chefs are used to cooking up whole calves!'

He had a cook summoned immediately and, without waiting for us, ordered him to slaughter the oldest pig. Then in a loud voice he said: 'Boy, which division are you in?'

When the cook replied that he was in 'the fortieth', Trimalchio asked, 'Were you bought, or were you born on my estates?'

'Neither,' said the cook, 'I was left to you in Pansa's will.'

'Better do a careful job,' replied Trimalchio, 'or I'll demote you to the messenger brigade.' The cook took the next course back to the kitchen, reminded of his master's power.

Trimalchio then gave us a friendly look and said, 'If you don't like the wine, I'll change it. It's up to you to do it justice. Thank god I don't buy it. Whatever makes your mouth water here is grown on some estate, which I haven't seen yet. It's supposed to be a spread in between Terracina and Tarentum. What I want to do is to add Sicily to my little holdings, that way if I want to go to Africa, I won't have to leave my own property!

'Now tell me, Agamemnon, what theme did you speak on today? Even if I don't plead in court myself, I did learn to read and write for home use. I'm no anti-intellectual. I own two libraries: one in Greek and one in Latin. So tell me, please, what was the theme of your speech?' 25

When Agamemnon had begun, 'A poor and rich man were enemies—' Trimalchio retorted, 'A poor man? What's that?' 'Clever!' replied Agamemnon, as he proceeded to explain some hypothetical case. Again, Trimalchio shot back a response, 'If this happened, it isn't hypothetical; if it didn't happen, it's nothing!'

We accorded these and other responses the most extravagant praise.

'My dear Agamemnon,' said Trimalchio, 'what do you know of the twelve labors of Hercules or the story of Ulysses and how the Cyclops got his thumb pinched in the tongs? As a boy, I used to read these stories in Homer. Yes, and at Cumae I saw the Sibyl with my own eyes hanging there in a bottle, and when some little boys asked her in Greek, "Sibyl, what do you want?" she replied, "I want to die!"'

Trimalchio was still chattering on like this when our table was covered by a tray with a huge pig on it. We were astonished by how speedily it had been prepared and swore you couldn't cook a run-of-the-mill rooster that fast, especially since the pig seemed much bigger than the boar that had been served a bit earlier. Then, looking intently at the pig, Trimalchio exclaimed, 'What is this? Has this pig been gutted? No, it hasn't, by god! Get that cook in here now!'

A contrite looking cook appeared in front of our table and admitted that he'd forgotten to gut the pig. 'What? Forgotten!' shouted Trimalchio. 'You'd think he'd forgotten to add the salt and pepper, the way he says it; off with his shirt!' In no time the poor man was stripped and flanked by two executioners. Everyone tried to get him off the hook saying: 'This happens all the time. Please, let him go. If it happens again, no one will speak up for him.'

Given my natural severity I couldn't resist turning to Agamemnon and whispering in his ear: 'This slave must be a perfect idiot: how could anyone forget to gut a pig? God knows, I wouldn't forgive him if he'd forgotten to clean a fish!'

Not so Trimalchio: his face relaxed into an hilarious grin as he said, 'O.K., since you've got such a bad memory, gut him right here in front of us.' The cook donned his tunic, again, grabbed his butcher knife, and sliced the pig's belly every which way with a quivering hand. The slits immediately gave way to the pressure from inside and roasted sausages and giblets gushed out of the wounds!

The slaves broke into applause for the trick and cheered in unison, 'Bravo Gaius!' The cook was honored with a drink and a silver crown, and also received a drinking bowl served on a plate of Corinthian bronze. As Agamemnon eyed the plate rather closely, Trimalchio observed: 'I alone own genuine Corinthian.' I was waiting for him to boast as usual that his vases were imported directly from Corinth, but he did better than that: 'Perhaps you're wondering why I am unique in owning Corinthian plates? Because, of course, the dealer I buy it from is named "Corinthus". How could it be Corinthian unless you get it from Corinthus? I'm no ingoramus, ya know; I know very well how Corinthian bronze originated. When Troy was sacked, Hannibal – a clever fellow and a real snake in the grass – piled all the bronze, gold and silver statues into a single heap and set them on fire. They melted into a single bronze alloy. From this amalgam craftsmen made little bowls, side dishes and statuettes. Thus was Corinthian bronze born – neither this nor that, but one from all. If you don't mind my saying so, I actually prefer glass – it doesn't smell. If it didn't break, I'd prefer it to gold; as it is, the price is right.

'But there once was a craftsman who made an unbreakable glass bowl. When he was given an audience with the emperor to present his invention . . . he had Caesar hand it back and then tossed it on the pavement. The emperor couldn't have been more alarmed! But his fellow picked the bowl up off the floor – it was dented like a bronze vase – pulled a hammer from his pocket, and smoothed it out very nicely. He thought he had Jupiter by the balls then, especially when the emperor asked, "Does anyone else know how to make glass like this?"

'But look what happened: he said "no" and the emperor had him beheaded! And no wonder! If an idea like that got out, our gold wouldn't be worth potter's clay!

'Of course, silver is my favorite. I have some enormous wine cups . . . showing how Cassandra killed her sons. The way the dead boys lie there – you'd think they were alive! I have a sacrificial bowl, which King Minos left my patron, that shows Daedalus shutting Niobe up in the Trojan horse. I even have the fights of the gladiators Hermeros and Petraites on my drinking cups – and, boy, are they heavy. You just can't put a price on that kind of thing.'

As he was talking, a slave dropped a drinking cup. Trimalchio glared at him and said, 'Quickly, off with your head, since you're good-for-nothing.' Instantly, the boy's face fell and he begged Trimalchio's pardon. 'Why do you ask me, as if I were your problem? I suggest you beg yourself not to be a good-for-nothing.' Finally, we prevailed on him to pardon the boy. As soon as he was off the hook, he danced about the table . . .

'Water for the outside, wine for the insides,' shouted Trimalchio, and we laughed approvingly at his jest, especially Agamemnon, who certainly knew how to get invited back to dinner. Feeling appreciated, Trimalchio drank happily and, when he was virtually drunk, said, 'Won't any of you ask my Fortunata to dance? Believe me, no one does the bump and grind better!'

He then held his hands up in front of his forehead and impersonated the actor Syrus, while the whole household chanted, 'Do it! Do it!' He would have taken the floor, if Fortunata hadn't whispered something in his ear. I imagine she told him that such clownery didn't become him. But nothing was so unpredictable: one moment he would cower before Fortunata, and the next, revert to his natural self.

The impulse to dance was checked by a clerk who read aloud as if from a government document:

'July 26th: on the estate at Cumae, which belongs to Trimalchio, there were born thirty male slaves, forty females; 500,000 pecks of wheat wre tranferred from the threshing floor to the barn; 500 oxen were broken in.

'On the same day, the slave Mithridates was crucified for speaking disrespectfully of the guardian spirit of our Gaius.

'On the same day, 10,000,000 in coin that could not be invested was returned to the strong-box.

'On the same day, there was a fire in the gardens at Pompeii that started in the house of Nasta the caretaker.'

'What's that? When did I buy gardens in Pompeii?' asked Trimalchio.

'Last year,' said the clerk. 'So they are not yet entered.'

Trimalchio was incensed: 'I forbid any property bought for me to be entered on the books unless I know of it within six months!'

Even the police reports were being read and the wills of some game-keepers, in which Trimalchio was disinherited in a codicil. The names of some caretakers followed and a divorce was announced – of a night watchman from a freedwoman: she had been caught *in flagrante* with a bath attendant. A porter had been exiled to Baiae; a steward was being prosecuted; and a law suit between some valets had been decided.

But finally, the acrobats arrived: some big lug stood there with a ladder and had a boy jump from rung to rung and dance a jig at the top. Then he made the boy jump through burning hoops, and pick up a large wine bottle with his teeth!

All this impressed Trimalchio alone, who kept saying, 'the arts are unappreciated.' But the two things he most enjoyed watching in all the world were acrobats and trumpeters; the other shows he thought were 'lightweight'. 'I even bought a troupe of professional actors,' he said, 'but I had them do Atellan farces and told my chorister to sing in Latin.'

Just as he was speaking, the acrobat . . . slipped and fell smack into our Trimalchio. The guests cried out as did the slaves, not on account of this pathetic creature whose neck they would happily have seen broken, but because it would spoil the dinner to end with a lament over a perfect stranger. Trimalchio himself groaned aloud and bent over his arm as if he'd been wounded. Doctors ran up, and leading the way was Fortunata with her hair down and a goblet in hand crying out what a poor, unhappy creature she was. The boy who had fallen was already crawling around our feet begging for mercy. What was worse, as far as I was concerned, was that these pleadings might be the set-up for some kind of joke: I still remembered the cook who'd forgotten to gut the pig. So I was looking all over the dining room to see what kind of jack-in-the-box was about to spring out at us, especially after a slave was beaten for dressing Trimalchio's bruised arm in white instead of purple wool! My suspicion wasn't misplaced: instead of punishing the acrobat, Trimalchio gave him his freedom! That way no one could say that a man of his stature had been wounded by a lowly slave.

We applauded his clemency and chatted about the mutability of fortune. 'We mustn't let this event pass without a trace,' said Trimalchio; he immediately called for writing paper and, with scarcely a moment's thought, composed these verses:

> Things always spin the way no one expects;
> Fortune on high all our affairs directs;
>   more good wine, boy, to counter these effects!

This epigram excited talk of poets, and it was maintained that the summit of poetry was held by Mopsus of Thrace, until Trimalchio said, 'Professor, how would you compare Cicero and Publilius the mime? In my opinion, the orator has more eloquence, the mime more nobility. What could be more ennobling than this?

> "Wanton jaws eat away at Mars' walls from within;
> peacocks fatten in cages for your palate's sin,
> sporting their gilded Babylon-plumes in the pen;
> with the capon ex-rooster, you cram Guinea's hen.
> Even storks, even those cherished guests from afar,
> family values' friends, shapely *chanteuses* that they are,
> runaways from cold weather and warrants of warm,
> take up nests in your fleshpots to their mortal harm.
> Why so value that fruit of the Indies, the pearl?
> So your wife tarted up like some crass glitter-girl
> can spread lecherous legs in another man's bed?
> What good that precious glass, those green emeralds,

that red,
that chalcedony gleaming like fire caught in stone,
unless what lends them luster is virtue alone?
Is it *right* when a bride flaunts a dress of thin air,
all decked out in sheer see-through, to strut her
    stuff bare?"

'Who do you think has the hardest job after writers?'
Trimalchio asked. 'I think doctors and moneychangers do.
Your doctor has to know what folks have in their insides
and when a fever comes on. I hate them though, because
they're always putting me on a diet. Your moneychanger's
job is hard because he has to spot the copper beneath the
silver. Now among dumb animals your hardest workers are
sheep and oxen: thanks to the ox, we eat bread; thanks to
sheep, we are clothed in glorious wool – it's a real crime to
eat lamb and wear shirts! But I think bees are divine creat-
ures – they vomit honey – even if some say it comes from Jove.
And that's why they have stings – because wherever
there is something sweet you'll also find something bitter!'

He was already putting the philosophers out of work
when little tickets were brought around in a bowl and the
slave in charge read out what the guests were given to take
home. *Pig in a Poke*: a ham was brought in under some
vinegar bowls. *Headrest*: a turkey neck was served up.
Hindsight and Insults: black-eyed peas and a plate of
tongue were the presents. *Something lean, something
mean*: the guest got a whip and a knife. *Sparrows and a fly-
catcher*: spare-ribs and Attic honey were served. *Something* 33

for dinner and something for business: a pork chop and writing tablets were brought in. *Something canine and something pedestrian*: a rabbit and a slipper were presented. *A catfish and a letter*: a cat was brought in with a fish tied to its back; beside it lay a dead bee. We laughed for ages at jokes like these, and there were scads more like them that I can't remember.

But when Ascyltos, unrul as ever, threw up his hands joking and laughing at everything until tears came to his eyes, he enraged one of Trimalchio's cronies (who was sitting right next to me): 'What are you laughing at, muttonhead? Isn't my master's entertainment good enough for you? I'm sure you're richer and used to better parties! So help me god, if he was sittin' next to me, I'd teach him how to bleat. A real wise guy, laughing at other people! Some fly-by-night bum who isn't worth his own piss! Listen, if I pissed around him, he wouldn't know which way to turn. By god, I don't have a temper, but maggots grow in rotten meat! He laughs: what does he have to laugh about? Did his daddy pay cash for him, is that it? So you're a Roman knight? Yeah, like I'm a prince!

' "*Then why were you a slave?*" 'Cause I wanted to be. I decided to be a Roman citizen, so I wouldn't have to pay tribute. And I hope the way I live now makes me nobody's fool. I'm a man among men, and I walk with my head up. I don't owe anyone a red cent. No, and I've never been sued. No one in the forum has ever told me, "Pay up!"

34   'Yeah, I bought some dirt and I've got my own dough

now. I feed twenty bellies and a dog. I even bought my wife, so no one could wipe his hands on her hair. And I bought my own freedom for a thousaand, and I was made a priest of Augustus free of charge. And when I die, I hope I won't have anything to blush about in the grave.

'Are you so busy you just can't see yourself? That's right, you see the lice on the other guy, but miss the flies on you. Only you think we're some kind of bad joke. Look, your professor here is older and wiser; he likes us. But you're still on the tit. You don't know your a's from your z's. You're a crock, no, a soggy shoelace – limper not better.

'Go ahead and live it up; have lunch and dinner twice a day. I wouldn't trade my good name for a million. Listen, did anyone ever have to dun me for a debt? I slaved away for twenty years, but no one could even tell if I was a slave or not! I came here a curly-haired kid. There wasn't even a town hall then. I just tried to please my master, a real gentleman whose little finger was worth more than all of you put together. Sure, I had some enemies at home who wanted to trip me up here and there. But I kept my head above water, thanks to my master. Now, these are real accomplishments. Hell, bein' born free is as easy as saying "I'll take one." Now, why are you staring at me like a goat caught in the garden?'

At this remark Giton, who was standing at my feet, erupted into a raucous cackle that he'd been trying desperately to stifle for some time. When Aschyltos' critic realized this, he 35 turned in rage at the boy: 'You too?' he said, 'you're laughing, you onion head? Well, whoopee! What is this, the Saturnalia? When did you pay your freedom tax? Ya know, you'll look good on the cross feasting crows. By god, I ought to give you hell, and that master of yours who won't keep you at heel! As sure as I get my belly full, I'd give you what for right here, if it weren't for my friend Trimalchio, a fellow freedman. We're all just having a good time but you freeloaders, well— Like master like slave, right?

'I'm really pissed off – I don't have a bad temper, but once I get started I don't give a plug nickel for my own mother! Damn right, I'm gonna find you on the street – you rat, you fungus! I won't budge till I've knocked your master upside down and inside out, an' I won't let you off if you scream bloody murder. I'll make sure your cheap curls and two-bit master won't save you then. Damn right, when I get my teeth into you, if I know me, you won't be laughin'. I don't care if you've got a beard of solid gold. I'm gonna give you hell – and that jerk who made you his step-and-fetch-it.

'No, I haven't learned your geometries, criticisms, or nonsense like "Sing the wrath" – but I can write in capitals n' do percentages in copper, weights, or cash. Listen, you and I can make a little bet, if ya want. Come on, I'll put down money. I'll show you your father wasted his dough teaching you rhetoric. Try this:

Of us I am, and *long* and *broad* involve me; solve me!

36 Here's a hint: what part of us runs and never leaves its

place; what grows out of us and becomes smaller? You look as scared n' confused as a mouse caught in a piss pot. So shut it up and don't bother your betters – who don't even know you were born! And don't think I'm taken in by those boxwood rings you swiped from your girlfriend. Heaven help us! Let's go into town and borrow some money, then you'll see what credit this iron ring of mine has.

'Shit! Ain't he a pretty sight – like a fox caught in the rain? I sure hope I don't get rich and die so happy that folks swear by my grave, if I don't hunt you down like a executioner. That master of yours sure is a pretty sight! What a teacher! Should a been a clown, not a professor. When we went to school the teacher used to say, "Your things in order?" "Go straight home!" "Mind your own business!" "Don't talk back!" But now, schools 've gone to hell. Nothin' worth a damn comes out of 'em. Thank god for my trade; it made me what you see.'

Ascyltos was about to answer this abuse when Trimalchio, delighted with the eloquence of his fellow freedman, said, 'Come now, let's stop this bickering! Let's enjoy ourselves, and you, Hermeros, forgive the boy. His blood's boiling – you should know better. The real winner is always the one who loses this kind of argument. Besides, you were a real cock-of-the-walk once and didn't have a grain of sense. So, it's better to start the party again and watch these rhapsodes perform.'

In trooped the actors at once amid a clatter of spears and   37 shields. Trimalchio was perched on his pillow, and, while the rhapsodes chattered to one another in Greek verse, as is their impudent habit, he read the Latin text aloud in a sonorous voice. Soon there was a pause, and Trimalchio said, 'Do you know what they're performing? Diomedes and Ganymede were two brothers. Helen was their sister. Agamemnon stole her and then gave Diana a stag instead. So now Homer tells how the Trojans went to war with the Parisians. Of course, Agamemnon won and made his daughter, Iphigeneia, Achilles' wife. That's why Ajax went crazy, as he'll explain in a minute!'

As Trimalchio spoke, the rhapsodes raised a shout and a throng of slaves carried in a boiled calf on a two-hundred pound platter. It was wearing a helmet. Ajax followed and, with his sword drawn as if in a fit of madness, he attacked the calf. Waving his sword up and down, he collected slices on its tip and then served them up to the astonished guests.

We didn't have long to admire this elegant performance: all of a sudden the paneled ceiling began to creak and the whole dining room trembled. I leapt to my feet in panic for fear that some acrobat was about to tumble down through the roof. The other guests also looked up in amazement wondering what novel portent was descending from heaven. And suddenly the ceiling *did* part, and an enormous hoop was lowered toward us. From its rim hung golden crowns and alabaster casks of perfume. We were being invited to take these as gifts when I looked back at the table . . .

A dessert tray loaded with little cakes had already been served. In the middle the baker had made a Priapus with all kinds of apples and grapes heaped in his ample lap in the popular fashion. We were greedily helping ourselves to this splendid offering, when a new game promptly rekindled our hilarity. As soon as any of the cakes or fruit was even touched, a saffron perfume spurted out – some of the damned juice squirted right in our faces. Thinking a dish so suffused with a religious aura must be a sacred offering, we leapt to our feet and shouted: 'God save Augustus, father of our country!'

Even after this ritual some guests were grabbing the apples. In fact, we filled our napkins with them, especially me, since I thought no gift too ample for me to stuff in Giton's pockets.

In the meantime three boys entered in short white tunics: two of them placed household gods adorned with lockets on the table in front of us; the third carried around a bowl of wine shouting, 'May the gods be gracious . . .'

Trimalchio said one of the gods was called Gain, the second Luck, and the third Profit. There was also a life-like portrait of Trimalchio himself, and since everyone else kissed it, we were too embarrassed not to do the same.

As soon as everyone had prayed for good sense and good health, Trimalchio looked at Niceros and said, 'You used to be livelier company. I don't know why you're so quiet. You haven't made a peep. Please, you won't see me happy until you tell us about that adventure of yours.'

Delighted with this attention from his friend, Niceros replied, 'May I never make another penny of profit if I'm not jumping for joy to see you in this mood. Let's have a real giggle – but I'm afraid your scholars here may laugh at me. Well, let them laugh. I will tell my story. What does it matter to me who laughs? As long as I'm laughed at, not laughed down.'

With these winged words, Niceros began his story:

'When I was still a slave we used to live in a narrow little street, where Gavilla's house is now. There, as the gods would have it, I fell in love with the wife of Terentius, the inn-keeper. You remember Melissa of Tarentum – what a luscious tomato! But I swear it wasn't her body or the sex that got to me but her good nature. Whatever I asked for, she never said "no". If she had two bits, I had one. Whatever I had I kept in her pocket, and she never cheated me. Now one day her husband died out at his master's estate. So I plotted and planned by hook or by crook to get to her: ya know how a friend in need is a friend indeed.

'Luckily my master went off to Capua to sell some nice junk. I grabbed the chance to get a house guest to come with me to the fifth milestone. He was a soldier and brave as hell. We push off around cockcrow; the moon was bright as daylight. When we get to a cemetery, my buddy takes off for some tombstones to do his business. I keep goin' just hummin' and countin' the stars. When I look for my buddy I see he'd stripped and piled his clothes by the roadside. My heart was in my mouth – I just stood there like a corpse. He pees in a circle round his clothes and then, just like that, turns into a wolf! I'm not kiddin' either; I wouldn't lie to you for anything. But, what I'm gonna say is, that after he turned into a wolf he started howling and then ran off in the woods.

'At first, I didn't know where I was, but then I go to pick up his clothes – they'd turned to stone! Was I scared, or what? I drew my sword and stabbed at shadows along the road till I got to my girlfriend's house. I walked in like a zombie and almost gave up the ghost then and there! The sweat ran down my crotch, my eyes felt dead. I could barely pull myself out of it.

'Melissa was surprised that I came so late: "If you'd come earlier, you could have helped us. A wolf got into the farm and attacked our flocks; he bled them like a butcher. He may have gotten away, but he didn't get the last laugh: one of our slaves speared him through the neck."

'I couldn't sleep a wink after I heard this, but at daybreak I hurried home like the defrauded innkeeper. When I came to the place where the clothes had turned to stone, I found nothin' but blood. But when I got home, my friend, the soldier, was lying in bed like an ox, and a doctor was treating his neck. I realized of course that he was a werewolf. After that I couldn't bring myself to eat with him, not on my life! Now I don't care whether you buy this or

41

not, but I'll be damned if I'm lyin'!'

The entire room was struck dumb with astonishment. 'With all respect for your story,' said Trimalchio, 'you can take my word for it – my hair stood on end, 'cause I know Niceros doesn't tell tall tales. No, he's real reliable, not a blabbermouth.

'Now I'll tell you something really scary – a regular ass-on-the-roof story. When I was still a long-haired boy – I lived like a Greek in those days – my master's favorite died. By god, he was a gem of a catamite, one in a million. Well, when his poor old mother was mourning him and several of us were grieving with her, some witches suddenly started to screech like owls – you'd think it was a dog chasing down a hare.

'At that time, we had a man from Cappadocia: tall, real brave, and was he strong! He could lieft an angry bull off the ground. This guy rushed outside with his sword drawn and his left hand carefully covered and ran a woman through right about here – may this spot I touch be safe! We heard her groan, but – see how truthful I am! – we didn't see the witches themselves. Our big lug came back in and threw himself on the bed; his whole body was black and blue as if he'd been flogged. Of course this was because the evil hand had touched him. We shut the door and returned to the funeral. But when the mother tried to hug her son's body, she reached out and found only a handful of straw! It had no heart, no innards, nothing. Of course the witches had already whisked the boy away and left a straw doll. Oh! you'd better believe it too: there really are witches, there are night riders, and what is high, they can make low. And that big lug never did look the same again. In fact, he died a raving lunatic just a few days later!'

We were as amazed as we were gullible. We kissed the table and prayed that these night riders stay at home – till we could get back from dinner . . .

To tell the truth, by this time the lamps seemed to multiply before my eyes and the whole dining room began to blur. Then Trimalchio said, 'Say, Plocamus, aren't you going to tell us a story? Won't you entertain us? You used to be a live wire, reciting dialogue and even an occasional poem. How sad it is! The ripe figs have fallen!'

'Yes,' he said, 'my life in the fast lane ended when I got the gout. But when I was younger, I almost wore myself out with singing. You name it: dance, dialogue, barber shop gossip! I had no peer except Apelles himself.' He then put his hand to his mouth and whistled some god-awful tune he later claimed was 'Greek'.

Not to be outdone, Trimalchio gave an imitation of trumpeters, and looked round for his favourite, whom he called Croesus. The boy with his bleary eyes and filthy teeth was in the process of wrapping a green handkerchief around an obscenely fat, black puppy. He then put a piece of half-eaten bread on the couch and proceeded to stuff it down the puppy's throat until it gagged. This inspired

Trimalchio to call for his own dog, Puppy, 'guardian of the home and family'.

A hound of enormous size was promptly led in on a chain, and, when ordered to lie down – with a swift kick from the steward – he sprawled right in front of the table. Trimalchio tossed him a piece of white bread and said, 'No one in my household loves me more!'

The boy was peeved to hear such praise lavished on Puppy, and so he put his pup on the ground and tried to get her to start a fight. True to his nature, Puppy promptly filled the room with his cacophonous barking and almost tore the head off Croesus' Pearl. The uproar didn't stop with the dogfight either: a candelabrum toppled over one of the tables shattering all the crystal and spattering some guests with hot oil.

Trimalchio tried to make light of the mess, kissed the boy, and told him to climb on his back. Croesus promptly mounted him like a horse, and kept slapping him on his back giggling and shouting, 'Bucca, bucca, guess how many fingers I'm holding up?'

After Trimalchio calmed down a bit, he ordered a great bowl of wine to be mixed and drinks served to all the slaves, who were sitting at our feet. 'And if anyone turns his drink down,' he added, 'pour it over his head: daytime is serious, now is for fun!'

This display of good nature was followed by a Greek
dessert, the very thought of which, frankly, is revolting.

Instead of the usual thrush each guest was served a fat hen and garnished goose eggs, which Trimalchio kept urging us to eat calling them 'deboned chickens'.

Meanwhile, an official's attendant knocked on the dining room doors and a reveller dressed in white came in trailing a large crowd of followers. His grand manner made me fear he was an important official. I started to get up and take off on my bare feet, when Agamemnon laughed at my panic saying, 'Calm down, you fool! Habinnas is an honorary priest and a mason best known for his tombstones.'

I sat down reassured by this news and greatly enjoyed watching Habinnas make his entrance. He was already drunk and ploughed along after his wife with his hands propped on her shoulders. A bunch of wreaths was piled on his head and scented oil streamed down his forehead into his eyes. He sat down in the seat of honor and immediately called for wine and hot water. Charmed by his high spirits, Trimalchio ordered a larger bowl of wine for himself, and asked how his friend had been entertained at another party.

'We had it all – except for you,' he said. 'My thoughts were here. But it was damn nice. Scissa was having a funeral feast for some poor slave she'd freed on his deathbed. That'll make a nice bundle for the taxman: they say the guy was worth fifty thousand. But it was swell, even if we did have to pour half our drinks over his little bones.'

'But what did you have for dinner?' asked Trimalchio.

'I'll tell you, if I can. My memory's a real marvel: constantly forget my own name. Well, for a first course we had a pig crowned with sausages and smothered in black puddings and gizzards roasted just right. And, of course, we had beets and pure whole wheat bread, which I like better than white: it gives you strength, and when nature calls, it doesn't hurt. The second course was a cold cheese tart and an excellent Spanish wine with warm honey in it. I didn't take a bite of the cheese tart but I soaked myself in the honey! There were chickpeas, lupines, a choice of nuts and an apple apiece. I took two myself and, look, here they are in my napkin. Ya see, if I don't have a present for my pet slave, there'll be trouble.

'Oh yeah, the boss reminds me: there was a hunk of bear set out, but when Scintilla tried it, she almost threw up her large intestine! But I ate almost a pound of it myself – it tasted just like wild boar. Yeah, I say if bears eat us men, why shouldn't men eat bears? We finished with cheese marinated in new wine, a round of snails, a bit of tripe, a little dish of liver, garnished eggs, some radish and mustard greens, a ragout, a dessert à la Palamedes. They even brought round a tub of pickled olives, which some folks were greedy enough to grab hand over fist. We had to pass up the ham.

'But tell me, Gaius, why isn't Fortunata here?'

'You know how she is,' replied Trimalchio, 'she won't let water touch her lips until she's gathered up the silver and divided the leftovers among the slaves.'

Habinnas responded, 'If she doesn't join us, I'm gonna push off.' He started to stand up when all the slaves chimed in on cue calling, 'Fortunata! Fortunata!' over and over again. She then made her appearance with her skirt hitched up by a yellow sash to reveal a cherry-red slip, ankle bracelets and gilded Greek slippers. She wiped her hands on a handkerchief tied around her neck, and then took her place on the couch, where Scintilla, Habinnas' wife, was reclining. Scintilla was clapping her hands as Fortunata kissed her and asked, as if in disbelief, 'Is it really you?'

Fortunata then went so far as to take the jewelry off her beefy biceps and show them to a duly impressed Scintilla. Finally, she even took off her ankle bracelets and golden hair net, which she said was solid gold.

Trimalchio observed these goings on and had the jewelry brought to him. 'You see these? A woman's chains!' he said. 'This is how we fools get plundered. She must be wearing six-and-a-half pounds of gold! I've even got an arm band myself that weighs almost ten pounds – all made out of what I owe Mercury!' Then, to show he wasn't lying, he had a set of scales brought in and passed around to test the weight.

Scintilla was no better. From her neck she took a golden locket, which she called 'Lucky'. From the locket she produced two earrings shaped like castanets, which she in turn handed to Fortunata for inspection. Then she remarked, 'Thanks to my husband's generosity, no one else has better ones.'

'What?' exclaimed Habinnas. 'You cleaned me out to buy a glass bean? You know if I had a daughter, I'd cut her ears off! If it weren't for women, we'd think this stuff was just a bunch of rocks. Hell, now we've got to piss hot and drink cold!'

Meanwhile the wives were getting sloshed, laughing together and exchanging drunken kisses. One chatted on about her virtues as mistress of the house, the other of the boyfriends and vices of her husband. While they gossiped, Habinnas quietly got up, grabbed Fortunata by the ankles, and swung her legs up on the couch. 'Oh no!' she shrieked, as her dress flew up over her knees. She then rolled over into Scintilla's lap and buried a hot blush in her handkerchief.

After a brief intermission Trimalchio ordered a dessert course served. The slaves took out the old tables and brought in the new, and they scattered sawdust tinted with saffron and vermillion, and – something I'd never seen before – a glittering powder made of mica. Immediately Trimalchio quipped, 'I just might be satisfied with these dessert tables alone – you all have your just desserts now! – but if you have something sweet, bring it on!'

Meanwhile an Alexandrian boy, who was serving the hot water, started imitating a nightingale, while Trimalchio kept shouting, 'Do something else.'

Then there was another gag: a slave who sat at Habinnas' feet suddenly began to chant the *Aeneid*, evidently at his master's request:

> Meanwhile Aeneas' fleet traversed the main . . .

A more disgusting sound has never assaulted my ears. Not only did he barbarize the pitch and rhythm of the verse, he also interlarded lines from the Atellan farces. For the first time in my life I actually found Vergil revolting. When he finally got tired and quit, Habinnas boasted, 'Can you believe he never went to school? I took care of his education by putting him out with the street people. He has no peer when it comes to mimicking mule-drivers or street musicians. He's damn clever: a cobbler, a cook, a baker, a real "slave of every muse". There are just two things that keep him from bein' one in a million: he's circumcised and he snores. Now I don't mind that he's cross-eyed. So's Venus. That's why he's never quiet: one eye is always on the move. I only paid three hundred for him.'

Scintilla interrupted this paean. 'You forgot to mention one of your slaves "muses": he's a pimp. And if I have anything to say about it, he'll be branded.'

Trimalchio laughed and said, 'Oh, I see. A Cappadocian, huh? He doesn't cheat himself out of anything, and I can't blame him for that: no one gives you a good time when you're dead.

'Now don't be jealous, Scintilla. Believe me, we know what you women are like. So help me god, I used to bang my mistress (and how!) until even the master got suspicious. 49

That's why he banished me to the farm. But be quiet, tongue, I will feed you.'

As if he'd just been praised to the skies, that worthless slave took a clay lamp out of his pocket and mimicked a trumpeter for more than half an hour, while Habinnas hummed along pressing his lower lip down with his hand. Finally, the slave strode into the middle of the room and did a flute-player with a handful of broken reeds. Then he donned a cloak and whip and did the *Life of a Mule-Driver* until Habinnas called him over, gave him a kiss, and handed him a drink. 'Bravo, Massa! I'm gonna give you a pair of boots!'

Our suffering would not have ended if a second dessert course hadn't been served: thrushes made of pastry and stuffed with raisins and nuts. Next were quinces bristling with thorns to look like sea urchins. All this would have been bearable if a more monstrous dish had not made us prefer death by starvation: what looked like a fat goose surrounded by fish and all kinds of birds was served. And Trimalchio said, 'Friends, all you see here is made of the same thing.'

Naturally wary, I immediately saw through the gag and, turning to Agamemnon, said, 'I'd be surprised if all this wasn't made from wax or clay. I saw this kind of fake dinner once at the Saturnalia in Rome.'

I hadn't finished speaking when Trimalchio said, 'As sure as
50 I hope to grow – in wealth not in bulk – my cook made this

whole course out of a pig! He's a rare talent: if you want it, he'll make a fish out of a sow's womb, a pigeon out of bacon, a turtledove out of ham, a chicken out of pork knuckles! And so I had the bright idea of giving him an artistic name: we call him Daedalus. And because he has good sense, I brought him a gift from Rome: knives made of Noric iron.' He promptly had them brought in and marveled at them. He even invited us to test the blades on our cheeks!

Two slaves stumbled abruptly into the room. They had evidently been fighting at the well. Anyway, they still carried large water jars on their shoulders. Trimalchio tried to adjudicate their quarrel, but they wouldn't listen to him. Instead, they smashed each other's jars with their sticks. Shocked by their drunken insolence, we couldn't take our eyes off the fight and noticed scallops and oysters pouring out of their broken jars, which a slave collected and brought around on a platter! The talented cook was equal to the occasion: he served us snails on a silver gridiron serenading us in a most repulsive, squeaky voice.

I'm ashamed to say what happened next. Following some unheard of custom, several long-haired boys presented us with ointment in a silver basin and rubbed it on our feet as we lay there after tying little garlands around our ankles and calves! Then some of the ointment was poured into the wine bowl and the lamp!

Fortunata was beginning to feel like dancing. Scintilla was already doing more clapping than talking, when Trimalchio said, 'Philargyrus, even though you're a notori- 51 ous fan of the Greens, you may sit down now, and invite your companion, Menophila, to join you.'

Need I say more? We were almost thrown off our couches, so completely did the entire room fill with slaves. Right next to me I noticed the cook who had made the goose out of pork – he reeked of pickles and sauces! Not content with having a place at the table, he immediately launched into an impersonation of the tragedian Ephesus, and then offered his master a bet that 'the Greens would win first prize at the games'!

Roused by this challenge Trimalchio said, 'Friends, slaves are human beings too and sucked the same milk as everyone else, even if bad luck has battered 'em down. But if I live, they'll soon get a taste of freedom. In fact, I'm setting them all free in my will! To Philargyrus I'm giving his farm and his bedmate; to Carion, I'm leaving an apartment house, his freedom tax, and a bed with blankets. I'm making Fortunata my heir and commending her to all my friends. And I'm doing it all up front – so my whole household can love me now just as if I were already dead!'

Everyone had started to thank their master for his generosity, when he turned serious and had a copy of his will brought in. He then read it aloud from beginning to end, while the slaves groaned as if in grief.

Then turning to Habinnas he said, 'Tell me, old friend, are you building my tomb just as I told you to? Please be sure that you put my lap-dog at the foot of my statue along with plenty of wreaths and jars of perfume, and all the fights of Petraites so that, thanks to you, I may live on after my death. And please make my plot a hundred feet wide and two hundred feet deep. For I want every kind of fruit tree growing around my ashes and lots of vines. It makes no sense to decorate the house you live in now but not the one where you'll spend so much longer. That's why over everything else, I want this inscribed:

THIS TOMB DOES NOT GO TO MY HEIR!

'But I'll make sure in my will that no one can wrong me when I'm dead: I'll appoint one of my freedmen to guard my tomb so that folks won't run up and take a crap on it!

'And please put ships in full sail on the front and put me high on a ceremonial dais wearing my purple-striped toga and five golden rings as I pour money out of a sack in front of the whole town – for you know, I once put on a public banquet that cost two-bits a head – and if it's all right with you, put some banqueting tables up there and show the whole town having a good time. On my right, put a statue of Fortunata holding a dove, and let the puppy follow tied to her sash, and include my favorite boy, and some giant jars of wine properly sealed against leaks, and you can carve one urn broken and a boy weeping over it. And put a sundial in the middle so whoever checks the time will read my name, like it or not! Now listen to this epitaph and tell me if it sounds right:

Here Lies C. Pompeius Trimalchio

Freedman of Maecenas,
Elected Priest of Augustus
In Absentia:
He Could Have Had Any Job in Rome –
But Didn't.

Loyal, Brave, and True,
He Started With A Nickel in His Pocket,
And Left His Heirs Thirty Million;
AND HE NEVER ONCE LISTENED TO A PHILOSOPHER!
Farewell, Trimalchio
And You, Too, Traveller.'

As he finished his epitaph, Trimalchio started to weep uncontrollably. And Fortunata wept. And Habinnas wept. And then all the slaves wept, as if invited to a funeral, filling the room with sobs. Even I had started to cry, when Trimalchio said, 'Well then, since we know we're going to die, why don't we try living? And since I want to see you happy, let's take a bath together! I swear you won't regret it: that water's hot as an oven!'

'That's right!' chimed in Habinnas. 'I like nothing better than making one day into two!' He then jumped up on his bare feet and took off after Trimalchio who was already cheery.

So I turned to Ascyltos: 'What do you say? I'll faint on the spot, if I even have to look another bath.'

'Let's play along,' he said, 'and while they're making their way to the bath, let's sneak out.'

We agreed to this plan, and Giton was leading us through the colonnade to the foyer, when the dog on a chain greeted us with such ferocious barking that Ascyltos backed into a fish pond! And I, who was no less drunk and had taken fright at a mere painted dog, was dragged into the same pool while trying to help Ascyltos paddle out. But we were saved by a porter whose intervention placated the hound even as he dragged us, shivering, onto terra firma. Meanwhile Giton had proceeded to buy off the watchdog with a clever trick: he had tossed the barker everything we'd passed along at dinner. The food had distracted him and muzzled his wrath.

But when, shivering wet, we asked the porter to show us out, he replied, 'You are wrong if you think you can leave the same way you came in; no guest has ever left the way he came in: they come in one way and go out another.'

What were we poor mortals to do trapped in this new-fangled labyrinth? Well, now we actually did want to bathe. So we asked the porter to lead the way, threw off our clothes, which Giton spread out to dry in the entry hall, and entered the bath. It was narrow, you see, and shaped like a cold-water cistern, with Trimalchio standing upright in it. We couldn't escape his mindless prattle even there. He was saying that nothing's better than bathing without a crowd, and that there used to be a bakery located on that very spot. Then, he got tired and sat down. Inspired by the echoing sound of the bath, he threw his head back, opened his drunken mouth, and massacred the songs of Menecrates. At least, that's what those who understood him said they were.

The rest of the guests joined hands and ran around the bath. The hall resounded with shrieks and giggles. Others tried to pick up rings off the floor with their hands tied behind their backs, or got down on their knees and tried to bend so far backward they could touch the tips of their big toes. While they played these games, we stepped down into a private tub that was being warmed up for Trimalchio.

So after we'd sobered up a bit we were led into another dining room, where Fortunata had set out every luxury . . . we noticed bronze statues of fishermen on the lamps as well as tables of solid silver decked with gilded chalices and wine decanted through a cloth filter right before our eyes.

Then Trimalchio said, 'Friends, a slave of mine is celebrating his first shave today. He's a good little crumb-saver, if I may say so, so let's drink deep and dine until dawn.'

While he was still speaking, a rooster crowed. Startled by the sound Trimalchio ordered that wine be poured under the table and that the lamp be sprinkled with unmixed wine. And he even switched a ring to his right finger. 'This is no coincidence,' he said. 'That rooster's giving us a sign. This either means there'll be a fire, or someone in the neighborhood is about to breathe his last. Spare us! Whoever brings me this prophet will get a tip.'

This was no sooner said than the rooster was brought in and Trimalchio gave orders for him to be cooked in wine. So he was butchered by that learned cook, who had earlier made fish and birds out of pork, and thrown in a cauldron. While Daedalus drank down the steaming broth, Fortunata ground up some pepper in a wooden mill.

When these savories were dispatched, Trimalchio looked at his slaves and said, 'Why haven't you eaten yet? Be off then, and let some others come to work.' So another team walked in, and, as their predecessors shouted, 'Good-bye, Gaius,' they shouted, 'Hello, Gaius!'

It was then that the party began to go sour. A handsome young boy turned up among our new waiters, and Trimalchio cornered him and proceeded to lavish kisses on him. To assert her wifely rights, Fortunata responded by bad-mouthing Trimalchio, calling him 'scum' and 'a disgrace' for not controlling his lust. Finally, she called him a 'dog'. Provoked by her abuse, Trimalchio threw his cup in her face. She screamed as if she had lost an eye and held her trembling hands to her face. Scintilla was also upset and sheltered her shuddering friend on her breast. A dutiful slave held an icy jar to Fortunata's cheek, which she leaned on as she moaned and wept.

But Trimalchio said, 'What's all this about? Has this whore forgotten where she was bought? I took her out of the gutter and made her fit for human society. But she puffs herself up like the proverbial bullfrog. She doesn't even spit in her bosom: a blockhead, not a woman! If you're born in a hovel, don't dream of palaces. I'll be damned if I'm going to give in to this "Cassandra in army boots".

And I could have married for millions, penniless as I was. You know I'm not lying. Agatho, the perfumer, took me aside just the other day. "I beg you," he said, "don't let your family die out." But good-natured fool that I am, I didn't want to seem fickle, so I stuck the axe in my own leg.

'Damn right, I'll make you want to dig me up with your own fingernails! And to show you here and now what you've done to yourself – now hear this: Habinnas, I forbid you to erect a statue of her on my tomb so at least I won't hear her nagging when I'm dead. And, so she'll know I can hit back – I forbid her to kiss me when I'm dead!'

When his fulminations ended, Habinnas tried to calm him down. 'No one's perfect. We're mortals, not gods.' Scintilla said the same thing through her tears and, calling him 'Gaius', begged him by his guardian angel to relent.

Trimalchio couldn't hold back the tears any longer. 'Please, Habinnas, as sure as you hope to enjoy your own nest-egg, spit in my face if I've done anything wrong. I gave the boy a very frugal kiss – not because he's beautiful – but because he's frugal! He can do division or read a book at sight; he saved enough from his daily allowance to buy a suit of Thracian armor! He's also bought himself an easy chair and two punch ladies! Now doesn't he deserved to be

the apple of my eye?

'But Fortunata forbids it! Don't you, my high-heeled Caesar? I warn you, magpie, enjoy what you've got! Don't make me show my teeth, lovebird, or you'll get a piece of my mind. You know me: when I make a decision, it's nailed to the ground. But let's remember the living!

'Please, friends, enjoy yourselves for I, too, was once what you are, but thanks to my native talents I ended up here. Brains make a man, the rest is garbage! I buy low and sell high. Everyone has his own pet wisdom, I guess. I'm just lucky as hell.

'Are you still crying, my snorer? I'll give you something to cry about.

'But – as I was about to say – frugality was the key to my success. When I left Asia I was no bigger than this candelabrum here. In fact, I used to measure myself by it every day and rub its oil on my lips to get a beard on my beak a little sooner! I was still my master's pet for fourteen years. To do your master's bidding is nothing to be ashamed of. And I gave my mistress equal time! You know what I mean. I say no more because I'm no braggart!

'Then I became the master of the house, as the gods willed; I simply had my patron in the palm of my hand. Why waste words? He made me his heir – along with the emperor – and I came into a senator's fortune. But no one is ever satisfied: I just loved doing deals. I won't bore you with the details: I built five ships and loaded them with wine – it was worth more than gold at the time – and shipped it to Rome. Every ship sank. You'd have thought I'd planned it that way. A fact, not a fable. On a single day Napture gulped down thirty million!

'Do you think I fell apart? No, by god, I didn't even blink. I built more ships – bigger, better and luckier! No one could deny I was tough. And you know, a big ship is tough too! I loaded them up again with wine, bacon, beans, perfume from Capua and slaves. This time Fortunata did the right thing: she sold off all her gold and all her clothes, and put a hundred gold pieces in my hand. This was the seed-money for my fortune. What the gods will happens quickly: I scooped up ten millions on a single voyage!

'I promptly bought back all the estates that had belonged to my patron. I built a house and bought up some mules and slaves. Whatever I touched grew like a honeycomb. Once I owned more than the whole country, I threw in the towel. I gave up doing deals and started lending money through my freedmen.

'I already wanted out of handling my own business, and a Greek astrologer named Serapa happened into our town and convinced me. He was on intimate terms with the gods. He even told me things about myself that *I* had forgotten. He explained me right down to my buttons: he knew my insides. The only thing he didn't tell me was what I'd had for dinner the day before. You'd have thought he'd always lived with me.

'Say, Habinnas – weren't you there when he said, "You

acquired your wife with your wealth." "You are unlucky in your friends." "No one ever returns your favors." "You own enormous estates." "You are nursing a viper in your armpit!" And something I should never tell you – right now I have thirty years, four months, and two days to live! And I shall soon come into a legacy. My horoscope says so. If I could only extend my estates to Apulia, I will have gotten somewhere in this life!

'At least I built this house while Mercury watched over me. As you know, it was a hut; now it's a temple. It has four dining rooms, twenty bedrooms, two marble colonnades, a series of servants' bedrooms, my private bedroom, this viper's lair, and a superb porter's lodge. And there's room enough for a hundred guests. In fact, when Scaurus visited here, he would stay nowhere else, and he has his father's place by the sea. There are lots of other things, which I'll show you in a minute.

'Believe me, if you have a nickel in your pocket, you're worth a nickel. You are what you own. Just like your friend – first a frog and now a king.

'Meanwhile, Stichus, bring out my funeral clothes – the ones I want to be buried in, and bring some perfume and a taste from that jar I want poured over my bones . . .'

Stichus didn't waste any time: he returned to the dining room carrying a white shroud and a purple-striped toga . . . Trimalchio urged us to feel if they were made of good wool. Then with a wily smile, he said: 'Stichus, make sure no mice or moths get at these – or I'll have you burned alive! I want to have a glorious funeral so that the whole town will shower me with blessings!'

He promptly opened a flask of exotic oil and anointed us all: 'I hope I like this as well when I'm dead as I do now!' He then had wine poured in a bowl: 'Now pretend you were invited here for my funeral banquet!'

The whole thing was getting positively nauseating when Trimalchio, now sloppily drunk, ordered some trumpeters into the dining room for more entertainment. Propped up on a pile of cushions he stretched out full length along the edge of the couch, saying, 'Pretend I'm dead: play something beautiful.' The trumpeters blared out a funeral march. One fellow – the slave of the undertaker who was the most respectable person there – played so loud that he woke up the entire neighborhood. This caused the local fire brigade to think Trimalchio's house was on fire. They promptly broke down the door and wielding axes and water proceeded to turn everything upside down, as usual. We seized this golden opportunity, gave some excuse to Agamemnon, and raced out of there as fast as if it *were* on fire.